LITTLE THINGS BETWEEN U & ME

KIERA GOPALIA

Copyright © Kiera Gopalia
All Rights Reserved.

to everyone lost in the dark. may you find your sun

Contents

Acknowledgements   *vii*

Guiding Light

His Pride

Home

Perfect

~

Safe Place

~

Origami

~

That Moment

~

Safe

Rest Of His Life

Highlighter

Smile :)

I Missed You

Airplane

Hope

This Feeling

~

Moon

Acknowledgements

Never wanted this book to be so formal, yet here I am... I really felt the need to acknowledge a few people that helped me a lot, throughout the book, who went through so much back and forth for me and for this book.

My mentor who guided me Mrs. Priya Narayanan, who helped me through every step of the way.

Mitra, Shivangi,Kamya and Tejal who gave me spiritual support everytime I hit a wall.

My parents who were with me from the beginning.

And to everyone else who supported me and helped me

:)

guiding light

you're watching me, i can feel it

your gaze constantly ablaze

i wish i knew where it was coming from so i'd know where
to look, because to me you're everywhere

when i wake, when i dream

the two lives separated by the seam, the seam of reality
and what we could be

when we're asleep shed some light for my soul, the lantern
which i hold, guides me to you

guides me home

his pride

"i'm proud of you, you know". you open your eyes to meet his large doe eyes staring back at you. his thumb brushes across your cheek softly. "what do you mean?" you ask as he replies with a soft smile playing on his lips "why can't i say i'm proud of you?" you kiss his palm and lean your face into his palm. "you're not getting the recognition you deserve, you're putting a lot of effort into everything you do and i'm very proud of you" he says, his smile widening. "i love u" you whisper as you pull him back to you on the bed smiling softly

home

they tell you "home is where your heart is" but they forget to mention that home can be a person, a memory, or even a song. i couldn't ever understand how anywhere except my own house was my home. that was until i met her. suddenly unexpectedly she began to fill my heart with a feeling, i couldn't quite describe. her smile can brighten any room no matter what length. her eyes pull me into the deepest trance falling over and under the waves of emotions i can't quite describe, ever.

the way she cares so deeply about things, moved me to new ends.

perfect

he watches you quietly as you stand in front of a mirror, the clothes you wore yesterday tossed on the floor beside you. his face softens as he takes in your red puffy eyes. he leans against the doorway rubbing your shoulder slightly "what's wrong" he asks you gently. you tell him, you tell him everything you're insecure about. you have never ever felt so unattractive before. he looks at himself in the mirror. "i hate my smile. i hate my face, it breaks out so often. my voice... it sounds like a broken cassette," he says ever so quickly. you can't hear anymore, so you put a hand on his arm looking at him with worried eyes. "what? why?" you tell him how someone like him has no flaws and how he's absolutely perfect

~

"why do you think you're any different?" you look at him confused not understanding what he just said. he continues and says "you ask me why i'm insecure about myself and how beautiful i am to you, how perfect i am but why do you feel you are any different, why is it when i tell you the same things they don't apply". you feel your shoulders fall. he takes your hand in his and says "you aren't perfect and once you'll fix something you're insecure about there will always be another" you don't understand why he's saying all of this, you didn't want to hear this… "you aren't perfect but you're still a piece of art, i find you beautiful baby, and i will always love you the way you are" he says and kisses your forehead. and for a moment it all becomes okay.

&

safe place

you walk out of his room, looking everywhere. you spot him walking towards you. you furrow your eyebrows attempting to read his expression. he comes near you he takes your shoulder and wraps his arms around your waist and finds a place in your neck, crying softly. he feels you wrap your hands around his neck and gently stroke his hair. his knees grow weak and he pulls you to the ground with him. he cries for a long time, you let him, you don't leave, you won't. he slowly lifts his head sniffling just enough to see your face as your soft eyes scan his face. he looks back down. you pull his head into your chest and kiss his hair. he hugs you once again, letting you hold him close.

~

he feels vulnerable in these moments, weak even. "you
make me feel safe" he says. "you didn't ask for
explanations, you didn't tell me to man up, you comforted
me, you never left and i never fear you will. you're my safe
place" he whispers. your heart warms up, you feel proud,
you were his safe place. you were glad he feels
comfortable around you.

origami

every morning you place an origami artwork on his desk, praying he would not notice you but on the other hand hoping he would. he is a popular kid and you wear specs, and had acne, two completely different people no? today you placed a heart on his desk, as soon as his friends saw the heart they started tossing it around laughing and making fun of him, you watch him get really angry and snatch the heart, only to place it in his bag carefully, you smile thinking even if this was anonymous, he treasured them. later that day as you come back from lunch he was sitting on your desk playing with the origami heart from earlier… "w-w-what are you doing here" you stuttered. "don't you want something in return?" he asked and you only shook your head vigorously in return. he chuckles at how adorable you are and says "too bad, i already made you something" as he takes out a poorly folded flower.

~

"I know it's not perfect, i'm sorry" he says before running off. you didn't mind, it was all okay, but what mattered the most was the thought and effort he put into it, you were glad you weren't invisible anymore. you keep the flower with you and keep it safe.

৪৩

that moment

"what was that moment for you?" you ask knowing he knows what you meant.

oh he knows the moment

"he sat in the living room with a few friends, eyes glued to the screen. he hears the door open and turns to see you walking in, he felt a smile grow on his face and he bite his lips to conceal it. he moves over making space for you to sit next to him. his friends look over and laugh to tease him he looked at them asking them to not embarrass him. he liked you. he liked you a lot. he had to tell you. a blanket rested over the two of you and you had one of your knees to your chest and the other leg was relaxed over the edge of the seat. he had his legs spread apart and his hand in a fist on his chest his heart was racing he was so close to you

~

*he didn't want to move, he didn't want YOU to move. as the
movie continued he grew impatient. he had to tell you. he had
absolutely no idea what the plot of the movie was, all he knew
was that you were enjoying the movie and he was happier to
watch you. instead he sat closer to you. your hand was resting
on your thigh under the blanket. he slowly slid his hand under
yours and interlocks your fingers with his. you close your
fingers in his hand smoothly. you see him smile from the
corner of your eye and bite the inside of your cheek to keep you
from smiling. you looked over and found his friends fast
asleep, you chuckled and rested your head on his shoulder as
his thumb stroked your knuckles. as he put his arms around
your shoulder he prayed you couldn't hear how fast his heart
was beating"*

that was the moment he said.

little did he know that was yours too.

৪৩

safe

he shifts in bed, his hand reaching out to you. you're not there. he sighs and sits up rubbing his eyes before staring at the wall adjusting to the darkness. you sat on the couch huddled in blankets, the lights were dim. nightmares were a part of your life for a long time. you felt like a burden to him, you didn't want to be the reason he slept late and woke up tired the next day. he saw you sitting on the sofa, he knew you had nightmares and he also knew you never woke him up because you didn't want to bother him, but he couldn't care less. he would do anything to make you feel safe at night. he picked you up and sits you in his lap, you hug him tightly. "i'm very sorry" you whisper. "i don't care if i'm up every night for you, i just hope i can make you feel safe love" nothing could make you feel safer. he was all you needed.

∞

rest of his life

you kept twisting and turning in bed, it was hard for you to sleep. his hands moved to your waist as he gently rubbed his hand over your skin and asked you in a raspy voice "what's wrong?" he generally slept well with you near, seeing you struggle only troubled him. you told him how you couldn't sleep and how you had stared at the pouring rain for hours but even that didn't help. "come here" he whispered. you lay your head on his pillow and draped your arm across his waist. he kissed your hair and began to sing. lips against your hair, he knew you found his voice soothing, you told him this time and again. he sang until he felt you sink in his hold. he stared at the ceiling smiling softly. he didn't mind singing you to sleep even for the rest of his life, all he needed was you beside him.

highlighter

"do you have a highlighter?" he asks. you shook your head and told him it was inside the room. he got up and got it, he continued reading the book. you watched him silently, raising an eyebrow when you saw him highlighting the novel. "what are you doing?" you questioned seeing him highlight another paragraph. he raises his head and says "everytime i read something that reminds me of you i highlight it". he stands up and heads to the bookshelf "pick one" he said. you opened a random book to see it highlighted in places. "they're all like this" he said. "at least the ones i've read after i met you" he smiles softly. he keeps his eyes on you, he saw you everywhere. you were his favourite story.

৪৩

smile :)

you put on a long t-shirt over your costume and walk out to the living room, you hear flopping in the hallway and you look over. he wore flippers on his feet and gigantic glasses on his face with the biggest smile ever painted across his lips. you throw your head back and laugh, he laughs with you. he removes the glasses and the flippers and kisses your cheek before saying "okay, we can go now, i just wanted to see you laugh". you tell him he did a good job and he smugly replies with an i know before cannonballing in the pool in the backyard. you get in with him and he asked "can we have a contest to see who can hold their breath longest?" with doe eyes. how could you refuse... you beat him

he let you

he liked seeing you smile.

∞

i missed you

it was late, you rubbed your eyes before finishing a report when your phone rang besides you, it was him. it had been months since you had seen him, you quickly put your specs back on and picked the call up. "what upppp" he said cheerfully. you smiled and said "all is good, but it would be better with you around" and pouted slightly. you asked him how his day was. it was interrupted by a loud knock on the door, you told him to hang on as you opened the door. and there he stood. phone in hand, he smiles and you run crashing into him. he laughed loudly and picked you up hugging you tightly. "i missed you" both of you said at the same time. you chuckle and get off but still hold his hands "i could do this all day" he said referring to the hug. "me too" you said and snuggled up close to him on the couch.

8

airplane

he yawns while waiting in line. he looks down, grabs your hand and kisses your head above the hoodie. he hands the tickets to the stewardess and walks on into the plane with you by his side. as you settle down he gives an earphone and puts the other in his own ear.

you listen to some music before you rest your head on his shoulder. "go to sleep baby, i'll wake you up when we pass something pretty". you smiled to yourself, he knew you liked looking at pretty things, just as he liked looking at you.

you listen to some music before dozing off on his shoulder his cheek resting on your head.

hope

you were silent for a while. he pulled back to look into your eyes, but you were covering your face with your hands and when he pulled back your fingers they were wet with your tears. he didn't prepare himself for this hug, so you knocked him onto the concrete so fast he had no option but to wrap his arms around you tightly. it was his first real hug after his brother had died. he didn't tell you, but in that moment - hugging you, comforting you... death didn't look as bad anymore. the future didn't look as bleak, because when you pulled back, when your eyes met his, he saw hope.

ଚଚ

this feeling

you sit atop a cliff, it's night time and the stars are brighter than usual. you look up in the sky filled with stars, almost as if they were smiling back at you. the ambience of the sea waves, accompanying your music but...you don't feel at home, tears slowly begin to roll down your cheeks. this feeling...this atmosphere where everything seemed at peace, *you feel happy. it would soon be over...once you take the leap, isn't that why you came here in the first place? to experience this one last time? but you can't seem to let this feeling go...can you? you would enter the void as you gazed at the starry sky, one last time. isn't that what we agreed on? so why won't you die?* as you began running towards the edge of the cliff, to cancel the strain that your emotions gave you, you suddenly stop. right at the edge,

~

cliched? of course. but you're still in love with this....this feeling. you know you can't feel this when you die. you sit back down on the edge legs dangling as you attempt to wipe the never ending stream of tears from your face. you gaze at the stars one more time. these stars...they gave you hope as they grew brighter in your eyes. the tears finally stopped as you lay down on the grass, the wind covering you like a blanket. "maybe I do have a reason for living on" you told no one in particular. you smiled the biggest smile you had in awhile. you're glad you chose to live on, as the sky brightens, the sun rises from the horizon with it's shine reflected by the sea.

୧୨

moon

and maybe i'll forget

maybe i'll make a promise and regret it

but in the end...

i think i'll always come back to you

because the thing is...

no matter how many mistakes i make,

you look at me like i hang the moon

৵০